AUNT
SEVERE
and the
TOY THIEVES

AUNT
SEVERE
and the
TOY THIEVES

NICK GARLICK
ILLUSTRATED BY NICK MALAND

Andersen Press
London

First published in 2013 by
Andersen Press Limited
20 Vauxhall Bridge Road
London SW1V 2SA
www.andersenpress.co.uk

1 3 5 7 9 10 8 6 4 2

British Library Cataloguing in Publication Data available.

ISBN: 978 1 849 39541 0

Printed and bound in Great Britain by CPI Group (UK) Ltd, Croydon, CR0 4YY

For Sandra Gillian Dixon
(1957–2011)

She would have loved the crocodile

1

Three Big Shocks

When he got up one morning, Daniel didn't know he was in for three big shocks by bedtime. He thought he was going to travel by train to the town where his Great-Aunt Emily lived, then stay with her while his parents went on to London. They were famous explorers and were off to the city to publicise a book about their latest adventures.

Daniel *did* get on the train. And he *did* travel across the country. Everything went as planned, right up to the moment he stepped down onto the platform and waved goodbye to his mum and dad.

That was when he got his first big shock.

Because it wasn't his Great-Aunt Emily waiting to meet him.

It was his Aunt Severe.

2
The Return of Aunt Severe

Aunt Severe actually *was* Great-Aunt Emily. She was his mum's auntie. But Daniel called her Aunt Severe because the first time he met her, she'd been a crabby old crackpot who fed him cold spinach sandwiches and woke him up at dawn to collect rubbish from the streets. Life with her had been grim and exhausting, and the only bright spot had been her kind and friendly next-door neighbour, the Colonel. When, after many strange adventures, the Colonel turned out to be her long-lost fiancé, she stopped being Aunt Severe and became a happy and giggling Great-Aunt Emily.

And that's who Daniel and his parents

thought she still was. It was certainly the way she'd been when they'd made the final arrangements for this visit.

But the woman waiting for him at the station wasn't happy. And she certainly wasn't giggling. She looked him up and down and frowned.

'I thought you'd be bigger,' she muttered. 'You've hardly grown at all.'

'It's only been five months, Aunt,' said Daniel, who was so startled by her unfriendly manner that he didn't know what else to say. 'I don't think anybody grows a lot in five months.'

'Stuff and nonsense!' said Aunt Severe. 'I expect you were just being lazy.'

She handed him a sheet of paper and a pencil and told him to write *I must be taller* five hundred and twelve times.

Then off she marched and not another word was said until they reached her house, which was just as dilapidated and broken down as the first time he'd seen it. That was when Daniel got his second big shock of the day.

'Where's the Colonel, Aunt?' he asked. 'Is he waiting for us at home?'

Aunt Severe fixed him with her most
forbidding glare.

'The Colonel,' she said, 'is not at home. He's
vanished again! He's vanished into *thin* air!'

3

A Strange Face

Since the Colonel's house was right next door to Aunt Severe's, she took Daniel inside to see for himself. All the rooms were empty. There wasn't a sign of the Colonel anywhere.

What Daniel *did* notice were piles of banana skins and empty sardine tins, mounds of little pebbles and lots of leaves missing from the Colonel's house plants.

Then Aunt Severe led him up to the spare bedroom and threw open the door. 'Look!' she boomed, 'at *this*!'

Inside, spread out on the shelves and tables, were battered tanks, deflated dolls, squashed cars, dilapidated trucks and rusty trains. There were rockets that wouldn't stand up, marbles that wouldn't roll and bricks that wouldn't build anything but rubble.

'This is all he left behind!' she said, waving her walking stick at the contents of the room. 'Nothing but bunkum and balderdash!'

Daniel was puzzled. 'Why was he collecting broken toys?' he asked.

'He said it was a surprise,' she replied. 'He said I'd find out soon. But now he's vanished without a word and I'm *most* annoyed!'

Daniel knew that the first time the Colonel had vanished, it hadn't been his fault. The army had sent him to guard a castle on the far side of the world and he'd been trapped inside by snow for twenty years. He'd never wanted to leave Great-Aunt Emily at all, and Daniel couldn't think of a single reason why he'd do it again.

'When did he leave, Aunt?'

'A week ago. I've been searching the whole town ever since. I'll find him, too. But until I do, I will be *most* annoyed!'

Daniel didn't answer, because he had just heard whispering in the bathroom. Yet when he looked inside, all he saw was a bath and a sink and towels on the rack. Then he saw the airing cupboard in the corner and realised that *that* was where the voices were coming from. But before he could open it, Aunt Severe led him back outside. Daniel told her what he'd heard but she wasn't interested.

'Hooey!' she said as she locked the front door. 'Claptrap and poppycock!'

And that was when Daniel got his third big shock of the day. Because, as they left and he looked back at the house, he saw someone peering down at him from a window.

It wasn't the Colonel, though.

It was a penguin.

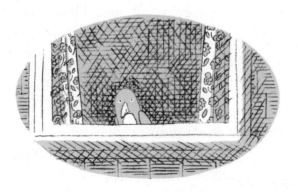

4

Spaghetti and Custard

Daniel immediately told Aunt Severe what he had seen but she refused to believe him.

'Tosh and tommyrot!' she replied, leading him into her house and down to the kitchen, where she handed him another pencil and another sheet of paper. 'Write *I must not talk tosh and tommyrot* six hundred and eighty-seven times!'

He sat and wrote out all his lines. When he was finished, she handed him a bowl of cold spaghetti and custard.

'No treats like spinach,' she said. 'It won't be a holiday like the last time you were here. When you've finished, you can write *I must not expect a holiday* three hundred and nine times.'

The next morning, it was even worse. Waiting for Daniel when Aunt Severe woke him up at dawn was a bowl of bananas and tomato sauce. And he hadn't even swallowed the last mouthful before she pulled on her overcoat, grabbed a map of the town and her walking stick and dragged him outside.

They set off through the dark, still streets and stopped only when they reached a tree-lined avenue on the other side of the town. Aunt Severe strode to the front door of the first house and rang the bell.

The owner appeared in his dressing gown and slippers, rubbing the sleep out of his eyes. Aunt Severe produced a photograph of the Colonel.

'Have you seen this man?' she demanded.

'It's six o'clock in the morning!' the sleepy owner protested.

'It's never too early to look for a missing Colonel,' said Aunt Severe.

But the owner had already banged his door shut and gone back to bed.

So it went at all the other houses in the area. Tired and grumpy people opened their doors, then slammed them shut when they realised what they'd been woken up for.

'Isn't it too early to be looking for the Colonel like this?' Daniel asked.

'Humbug!' said Aunt Severe. 'I started looking for him the day he vanished and I intend to get up every day at dawn and search every house in every street in every town in the country if I have to. I'll find him wherever he is! Do you still have your pencil?'

'Yes, Aunt.'

'Good,' she said. 'Start writing *My aunt will find the Colonel wherever he is!* until I tell you to stop. And don't forget the exclamation mark!'

She pulled the map from her pocket and crossed off all the streets and houses they'd just visited.

'Are we going home now?' asked Daniel. From the moment he'd woken up, all he'd wanted to do was get into the Colonel's house and find the penguin.

'We most certainly are not!' said Aunt Severe. '*Now* we go to the police!'

5

Slither and Lurk

When they reached the police station, Aunt Severe handed the officer on duty a picture of the Colonel. He sighed when he saw her come in and he sighed as he put the picture with all the other pictures of the Colonel piled up on his desk.

'Have you found my fiancé?' she asked.

'No, madam,' he replied. 'But we are still looking.'

'Obviously not hard enough,' said Aunt Severe. She gave him a sheet of paper and a pencil. 'Write *I must look harder* two hundred and seventy-two times.'

Then she demanded to see the Superintendent.

Daniel groaned. At this rate, he'd *never* find out about the penguin. To give himself something to do, he started looking at all the posters on the wall. One in particular caught his eye.

WANTED!

International toy thieves!

Lionel Lurk   **Sidney Slither**

No toy safe
from these two!
Be on the lookout!
HUGE REWARD
for their capture.

WANTED! it said in great big bold letters. *International Toy Thieves!*

Below the words were two photographs. One showed a tall and gloomy-looking man with big feet and long fingers. His name was Lionel Lurk. The other showed a short and thin individual wearing an enormous pair of sunglasses. He was called Sidney Slither.

'There isn't a toy in the world safe from those two,' said the policeman at the desk.

'Really?' said Daniel.

'Stolen toys from everywhere, they have. The Duke of Argentina's children's Christmas presents. The Queen of Iceland's toy horses. The Count of Australia's clockwork-mouse collection. Last week they even broke into the Prime Minister's holiday home and ran off with all his son's video games. And that's not to mention all the shops, schools and museums they've plundered.'

The policeman pointed at the photo of Lionel Lurk.

'See those fingers?' he said. 'Just right for picking locks and reaching through half-closed

14

6

A Pink Plastic Crocodile

Once they got home, Aunt Severe served Daniel a plate of soggy sprouts and ice cream made from mustard before settling down in her favourite armchair. He could see she was tired after the morning's walking, so he wasn't surprised when she closed her eyes and dozed off. Seizing his chance, he took the key to the Colonel's house from her overcoat pocket, tiptoed outside and ran next door.

The first thing he saw when he let himself in was a pink plastic crocodile, lying on the carpet by the staircase. Just as he was about to take a closer look, he heard chewing coming from the dining room. So he opened the door to see what was making the noise and almost jumped out of his shoes. Opposite him, nibbling away at the leaves of the plants growing in pots on the windowsill, were two ostriches with very long necks.

The second they saw Daniel they stopped eating and shot under the dining table. They curled up into tight little balls with their beaks buried beneath their bodies, trembling like jellies in an earthquake.

'I won't hurt you,' Daniel said, when he'd got over his shock. 'Really I won't.'

Nothing he said could calm them down, though, so he left them alone and went back to the plastic crocodile. But before he got there, he was distracted by the sight of three monkeys sitting on the sofa in the living room, munching bananas. They had red backs, white tummies, long legs and even longer tails. He was so startled he stopped and stared, at which point all three monkeys spotted *him*, flung their food away and tried to escape.

The monkey on the right jumped left. The monkey on the left jumped right. This led to a fearful crash as they both collided with the monkey in the middle. Clutching their heads in pain, they fell off the sofa and collapsed in a heap on the carpet. When Daniel went to help, they crawled under the sofa and refused to come out.

He was thinking that he'd seen the ostriches and the monkeys somewhere before when he heard a new noise. It sounded like bedsprings creaking and it was coming from above. Stepping over the pink plastic crocodile, he climbed the stairs and peered round the first door he came to.

Inside, bouncing up and down on a bed, was the penguin. It was small and plump and far too busy eating sardines from an open tin on the pillow to notice Daniel. Each time it landed on the bed, it snatched a sardine from the tin and gobbled it down.

Daniel stepped back onto the landing, only to see the monkeys and the ostriches huddled together at the foot of the stairs, right behind the crocodile. All six animals were staring at him.

And then the crocodile opened his mouth and spoke.

'I bet you thought I was plastic,' it said.

7

A Very Talkative Penguin

Daniel jumped again, higher than ever this time.

'You can *talk*!' he said.

'We can *all* talk,' replied the crocodile.

'And *you're* a real crocodile,' he added.

The crocodile sighed. He looked very sad. 'You *did* think I was plastic,' he said, 'didn't you?'

Daniel nodded. 'Sorry,' he said.

'That's OK,' the crocodile muttered, 'I thought you would. Did you ever see that other one in the cage with me, out there in the zoo?'

During Daniel's first visit to Aunt Severe, he'd discovered a zoo – a very small zoo – on the other side of the fence at the bottom of her garden.

It was owned by a mean old man called Gotcha Grabber, and into it he had crammed four small cages stuffed with all sorts of animals. One of them, Daniel remembered, had contained six penguins, a hippopotamus, and two crocodiles. The other cages, Daniel realised, were where he'd first seen the ostriches and monkeys.

'Yes,' he said, walking downstairs. 'I did. I thought you were plastic then, too.'

'The other crocodile was the plastic crocodile,' the pink crocodile said.

'It didn't *look* plastic,' said Daniel.

'That's why Gotcha Grabber bought it,' the crocodile replied. 'He said nobody would be scared of a pink crocodile. And he was right. All the visitors thought I was a toy and they weren't frightened of me for so much as a second. If you're a crocodile, that's *really* depressing.'

He laid his head flat on the carpet and gazed glumly at the wall.

Daniel looked at the animals. 'How did you learn to talk?' he asked.

'Oh,' chirped a cheerful voice from behind him, 'that was me.'

Standing at the top of the stairs was the penguin. He had a black back, a white tummy and tiny white rings around each eye. He hopped down the stairs towards them, and as he hopped, he talked.

'*I* learned how to speak People first, and then I helped the ostriches and the monkeys and the crocodile speak People, too. I like helping. Helping is *fun!*'

He stopped on the bottom step and gave Daniel a curious look.

'You don't say very much, do you?' he said.

'I was waiting for you to stop talking,' replied Daniel.

'Oh,' said the penguin. 'Penguins *never* stop talking. We're *always* talking. There's so much to say and we say it. Do *you* have anything to say? If you don't, just let me know and I'll think of something for you. It won't take me long. It never does.'

'I have something to *ask*,' said Daniel.

'That's even better!' the penguin replied. 'Is it an interesting question? I like interesting questions. Actually, I like all kinds of questions because I get to answer them. But an interesting question is the best kind of question because then I get to give a really interesting answer. Do you know—?'

'*How* did you learn to talk?' Daniel interrupted. 'And what are you doing here, in the Colonel's house?'

'*Two* questions!' the penguin cried, flapping his flippers happily. 'That means *two* answers! Oh, this really is excellent! The dragons did it.'

As startled as he'd been by finding the animals in the Colonel's house, Daniel wasn't surprised to hear of dragons. When he'd first stayed with Aunt Severe, he'd found four of them hiding in a tree in her back garden. That was just before evil Gotcha Grabber kidnapped and put three of them on display in his zoo. But with the aid of the fourth dragon, the Colonel and Aunt Severe, Daniel had managed to rescue them all. And it was during those adventures that Aunt Severe had been reunited with the Colonel and returned to being happy and giggling Great-Aunt Emily.

'What did the dragons do?' he asked.

'Taught me the spell that let me speak People,'

said the penguin. 'I *do* hope they're coming back. I'll bet there's all sorts of other things they could teach me and I'd certainly like to learn. I like learning. If I were a people like you I'd love to go to school and learn all day. That would be marvellous.'

'Why did they teach you the spell?'

'I asked them to. When they were locked up next to me, I heard them say they'd been talking to a people, so I asked them to teach me how to do that. And I kept asking until they did. They were ever so—'

'But what are you all *doing* here?' Daniel interrupted. 'In the Colonel's house?'

'Oh,' said the penguin, waving a flipper at the other animals, 'that's simple. They're all here because they're useless.'

And one by one, the other animals sadly nodded their agreement.

8
Useless

'*Are* you useless?' Daniel asked.

'Completely,' sighed an ostrich.

'Utterly,' muttered a monkey.

'Completely *and* utterly,' moaned the crocodile.

'You don't *look* useless,' Daniel said.

'Really?' said one of the ostriches, 'What about this, then?'

She stretched her neck out and then up, up and even higher up until her head touched the ceiling. Her sister did the same.

'Ostriches,' she said, 'have long necks so they can spot dangerous animals when they're out on the plains. But if you've got necks as long as *ours*, then all the dangerous animals can see *you* first.

So none of the other ostrich flocks wanted us around. They said we were bad luck and chased us away. And when we were all alone with our big long necks, it was ever so easy for the hunters to spot us and capture us and send us here. We're definitely useless.'

'We're clumsy,' said a monkey. 'We're always bumping into things.'

'All we can do is hold tight,' said the second monkey.

'And that's not very useful when you're meant to go swinging through the trees,' the third monkey said. 'We end up stuck to the branches. It's why we were so easy to catch.'

'What about you?' Daniel asked the penguin. 'Why are you useless?'

'I'm *not*!' replied the penguin. 'I'm as perfect a penguin as a penguin could be. I just stayed here to help my friends speak People. I like helping. I like it almost as much as talking.'

'I wish you'd help us by shutting up sometimes,' a monkey muttered.

The other animals wearily nodded their agreement. The penguin looked offended, but

before he could answer, Daniel turned to the
crocodile.

'And you're pink,' he said.

'Oh, that's right,' the crocodile grumbled. 'Rub
it in. Make me feel even worse. You might as well
say something about my teeth while you're at it.'

He opened his jaw to reveal rows of teeth. They
weren't sharp and pointed, like normal crocodile
teeth, but round, like the end of a blunt pencil.

'A pink crocodile with round teeth,' he said. '*Nobody's* scared of that!'

He put his head on the carpet and closed his eyes. One of the monkeys patted his back. The ostriches covered him with their big fluffy wings. But it only cheered him up a little bit.

'That's why we hid when the people persons came to look at us.'

'What people persons?' Daniel asked.

'The people persons who came to take the other animals back home,' the penguin said, happy to be talking again. 'Do you remember when the dragons left, your aunt and the Colonel decided to look after the zoo?'

Daniel nodded.

'Well, they did. But all the while they were looking for ways to help us go back home. They didn't want to keep us cooped up here in such a tiny space. And it was costing them all their money to look after us. They couldn't even afford to repair your aunt's house. So the owls went off to a forest in Scotland. The kangaroos went back to Australia. The porcupines flew off to North America, the camels to Morocco and the parrots to Brazil. And the hippopotamus, the giraffes, the baboons and the elephant all sailed away on a ship to somewhere else in Africa. They *all* went home!'

'Soon there was nobody left but us,' an ostrich said.

'But we didn't *want* to go back,' the monkeys added. 'We didn't want to be laughed at by the other animals when we got there.'

'Mr Colonel didn't laugh at us,' the crocodile explained. 'He said he'd look after us all and we could stay with him if we wanted to.'

'That's why we like Mr Colonel,' added the ostriches and the monkeys.

'Then where *is* he? Daniel asked. 'What happened to him?'

'Oh,' said the penguin cheerfully, 'he's been kidnapped. I bet that's really interesting, being kidnapped.'

Daniel couldn't believe his ears. 'Kidnapped? Who kidnapped him?'

'Two people persons,' the penguin said. 'One was tall and thin and the other was round and short.'

Daniel immediately thought of the *WANTED* poster in the police station. 'Did the short one have great big sunglasses?' he asked.

All the animals nodded and Daniel was so confused he didn't know what to think. Why had international toy thieves kidnapped the Colonel?

The penguin was only too delighted to explain.

9

A Very Happy Colonel

'It all began a week ago,' the penguin said. 'Your aunt was away looking for new homes for us and Mr Colonel came to give us our breakfast. I'd been practising People really hard by myself and I thought it was time to start talking it with an actual people person. So I said *Good morning.*'

'What happened?' Daniel asked.

'He dropped the buckets he was carrying, sat on the ground and said "*Blow my chimneys down! You're talking!*" So I told him "*Yes, I was talking, because talking was fun and I wanted to do lots more and could I do talking with him?*"'

'And—?' said Daniel.

'And then I explained about the dragons and

the spells and learning to speak People. And since the Colonel knew all about the dragons, he wasn't really very surprised, not even when I told him the ostriches and the monkeys and the crocodile could speak People, too.'

'So—?' began Daniel.

'So then I asked him why he was so happy and could I see inside his house, because I'd always been curious about people houses. And that's when we found out Mr Colonel was ever so nice because he took us *all* inside and listened to *all* our stories and said if we didn't want to go home then we could stay with him.'

'Then—?' tried Daniel for the third time.

'Then he took us to the spare bedroom. It was full of broken people toys. He said your aunt had found them when she collected rubbish and had never thrown them away. He'd decided to tidy them up, but he'd stopped when he found something that *wasn't* rubbish. He said it was the princess and that the reward for finding her was going to pay for your aunt to rebuild her house. *And* keep us here, too. He said he'd sent the princess to the National Gallery in London.'

Daniel couldn't stop the words bursting out. 'What was a princess doing in my aunt's attic?'

'Honestly!' the penguin complained, 'I'll *never* finish my story if you keep interrupting like this. Mr Colonel said it was the Princess of S—. But he didn't tell us the rest.'

'Why not?'

'Because someone knocked on the door and he went downstairs to see who it was. We heard shouts and went out onto the landing and there was Mr Colonel was in the hallway, struggling with the tall people person and the short people person. They kept asking where the princess was, and Mr Colonel said she was in London.'

Then the penguin fell silent and all the animals looked downcast.

'What happened?' Daniel asked.

'We tried to rescue Mr Colonel,' the crocodile said. 'And everything went wrong.'

10

Kidnapped!

'What did you do?' Daniel said.

The ostriches, the monkeys and the crocodile all turned to the penguin.

'*He* did it first!' they said.

'I was only trying to help,' the penguin said. 'I thought I could think up a spell. After all, a dragon spell taught me to speak People, so I thought I'd try one to save Mr Colonel. And it did work. At least a little bit.'

'The *little* part did,' the crocodile muttered. He turned his sad eyes to Daniel. 'The spell didn't *rescue* Mr Colonel. It made him *smaller*. And then smaller still. He only stopped getting smaller when he was the same size as the penguin.'

'What about Slither and Lurk?' Daniel asked. 'Were they frightened?'

'Not a bit,' said the crocodile. 'They thought it was funny. They started throwing Mr Colonel back and forth and up into the air and the smaller he got, the happier they were. They said he was the perfect size for climbing down chimneys and crawling through tiny windows. They said they could use him to steal tons of toys on the way to London! *And* help them steal the Princess. That's why they'd come here in the first place: they'd heard about him finding her.'

'Then they looked at *us*,' continued an ostrich, 'and laughed even harder. They said they'd never seen such a useless bunch of animals in their lives. So me and my sister tried to rescue Mr Colonel. But we forgot how long our necks were. I got mine tangled in the chandelier and she got hers caught in the overcoats by the door. We really were useless.'

'We were even more useless,' said a monkey. 'We managed to get outside, but that was all. I banged my head on the door handle. My brother tripped over me and fell on his tummy. And then our other brother fell over us both and landed up on his back in a rose bush.'

'I got outside, too,' the crocodile said. 'I told the thieves I'd eat them if they didn't put Mr Colonel down. But all they did was laugh and shove me in a sack because they thought I was a talking toy. They weren't scared for a second.'

'That's really, really rotten!' Daniel said. 'There you were trying to be brave and they just laughed at you all. That must have been awful!'

'They thought I was a toy, too,' the penguin interrupted. He obviously didn't want to be left out of the story. 'They put me in the sack with the crocodile and put us in their car. Then it got really interesting, because the sack fell open and I jumped out and said I'd never been in a car before and asked them if driving was complicated and could I learn. I told them I *liked* learning.

'But they didn't answer, so I hopped onto the dashboard and peered through the wind-screen. I asked them if we going somewhere interesting. I told them I liked interesting places. I said I started out in Antarctica and that it was really interesting. Then I asked them where the most interesting place was they'd ever been?

'And then it got even better because the tall people person picked me up and threw me onto the back seat and I realised you could see through the rear window, too. You could see where you were going *and* where you'd been! And both at the same time! That was *ever* so interesting. I knew I was really going to like driving!'

The penguin stopped and looked puzzled.

'But they didn't take me with them,' he said. 'They picked me up and dropped me on the pavement. And do you know what they said? They said they weren't going to listen to *me* all the way to London, which I thought was really silly because I had *such* a lot of interesting things to tell them.'

Daniel looked at the crocodile. 'Did they throw you out, too?' he asked.

The crocodile nodded. 'They said they'd decided they didn't need a boring plastic crocodile. And then they drove off with Mr Colonel.'

'What did you do then?' Daniel asked.

The crocodile looked glum.

'I said, *I thought that would happen.*'

11
A Third Toy Thief

When the stories were all over, Daniel sat down at the bottom of the staircase and thought about what he'd heard. It didn't take him long to decide what to do.

'We have to tell my aunt,' he said.

Just the thought of telling Aunt Severe made every animal run off and hide. Except the penguin.

'Oh, goody,' he said. 'I *like* telling stories.'

'No!' screeched an ostrich, poking her head out from under the dining room table. 'That's why we all hid in the bathroom whenever your aunt came round. So she *wouldn't* find out we lost Mr Colonel.'

Ever so patiently, Daniel coaxed the animals back into the hallway.

'*I'll* tell my aunt,' he said. 'And I'll make sure she knows you tried to stop him being kidnapped.'

'Doesn't she frighten you?' asked a monkey.

'She does a bit,' said Daniel. 'But if I don't tell her, she won't be able to rescue the Colonel. And we can't let that happen, can we?'

The animals all reluctantly agreed.

'We like Mr Colonel,' the crocodile said.

So Daniel took a big deep breath and started towards the door. But at that precise moment, it swung open and a shadow fell across the hallway. It was Aunt Severe, looking as severe as Daniel had ever seen her.

'And just *what*,' she demanded in an icy voice, 'is going on here?'

'Oh,' said the penguin, 'I can tell you *that*.'

And before anyone could stop him, he promptly rattled off everything that had happened – right from the moment he'd first spoken to the Colonel and all the way up to Aunt Severe's arrival.

'Isn't that *interesting*?' he finished. 'By the way, is that a walking stick you're carrying?

Can I have a go? A penguin with a walking stick would look *really* interesting!'

There was a cupboard under the stairs. Aunt Severe put the penguin inside and closed the door.

He was silent for only a moment.

'Gosh,' everyone in the hall heard him say. 'I've never been in here before. It's fascinating! I think I *like* cupboards.'

Aunt Severe ignored him and turned to the others.

'Let me sum up,' she said. 'There was a princess in this house. The Colonel has been kidnapped by toy thieves. He's now the size of a penguin and has gone to London. We do not know where in London and *I* am *most* annoyed. There's obviously only one thing to do.'

Before anyone could utter so much as a squeak of protest, she prodded them all – including the penguin – out through the door and off to the police station to tell the Superintendent.

But they never set foot inside because, as they approached the building, Daniel spotted a new poster pinned to a notice board by the front door. It was a picture of Sidney Slither and Lionel Lurk, running away from a toy museum near London. In their arms was the Colonel, clutching a bag of dolls. Daniel could hardly believe what he was reading:

HAVE YOU SEEN THIS MAN?

New thief joins
Slither and Lurk gang.
Your toys even less safe!

Daniel ran after Aunt Severe and stopped her on the steps to explain what he'd seen. 'And you're the Colonel's fiancée,' he finished. 'If you go inside, the police might think you're a member of the gang and arrest you, too. Then you'd never get him back.'

45

'That,' said Aunt Severe, 'is a surprisingly excellent point!' She handed him a sheet of paper and a pencil and told him to write *I must make more excellent points* six hundred and seventy-two times. Then she turned to the animals and said, 'If the police cannot help, we will have to get the Colonel back ourselves.'

She promptly herded them all off to the nearest bus stop.

'Nine tickets to London,' she said when the bus arrived.

'Sorry,' said the driver. 'No animals on board.'

That didn't bother Aunt Severe. She marched them all to the nearest taxi rank. But every driver said the same thing.

'I'll take you, the boy and the plastic crocodile. But not those animals.'

Aunt Severe remained unperturbed. 'Very well,' she announced. 'We will take the train!'

'We can't get on a train, either!' the ostriches said.

'We're *animals*,' the monkeys added. 'They won't let us on board.'

'They might if you have disguises,' said Daniel. He wasn't going to let anything stop them rescuing the Colonel.

Aunt Severe agreed and set off for home. The animals plodded sadly along behind her, with the crocodile gloomily bringing up the rear.

'I thought that would happen,' he muttered.

12

Disguises

Once inside, Aunt Severe lined up the animals in a row and studied them carefully. She said 'Hmmm' a lot. Then she took down the curtains and placed them on the table.

'Interesting,' said the penguin.

The ostriches and the monkeys crept off to hide under the stairs. Aunt Severe found them and sent them up to her bedroom, where she rummaged around collecting hats and scarves.

'This is interesting, too,' said the penguin, waddling along behind.

While she was doing that, the ostriches slid under the bed and the monkeys climbed into a drawer. Aunt Severe dug them out and took them to the attic. As she pulled boxes off shelves, dust flew up in clouds and spiders and cobwebs went sailing in every direction.

When she finished, she had filled a large wooden crate, which she told Daniel to carry down to the living room. Then she stepped back into the attic, tipped the ostriches and the monkeys out of an old trunk and led them downstairs. Daniel and the penguin examined the contents of the crate.

It contained two pairs of sunglasses and two straw hats, three old anoraks, a woollen cap and scarf, a suitcase handle, a roll of sticky tape, three wobbly roller skates, a red ribbon and a ping-pong ball with a hole in it.

'This is *very* interesting!' the penguin said. 'I can't wait to wear *my* disguise!'

Aunt Severe set to work sewing and folding and gluing. Then she stopped and looked at the animals.

'I don't know your names,' she said. 'What are you all called?'

The animals hung their heads and looked embarrassed.

'I can't go around saying *Ostrich* and *Monkey*,' said Aunt Severe. 'No one will know who I'm talking to and there will be chaos. I do not like chaos! It makes me *most* annoyed!'

Finally, the crocodile answered. 'We haven't got any.'

'Bilge and blather!' said Aunt Severe. 'Everyone has a name.'

'Not us,' said the crocodile. 'You don't get a name if you're useless.'

'*You* could give us a name,' suggested an ostrich.

'I bet you know lots,' said the monkeys.

'Well,' said Aunt Severe, thinking it over, 'my mother was called Hermione—'

'Wonderful!' cried the monkeys and the ostriches. 'You can call us Hermione!'

'I can't call you *all* Hermione,' said Aunt Severe.

'We heard it first!' the ostriches said.

'*We* did!' said the monkeys.

'We're *bigger* than you!' the ostriches said.

'But there's only two of you,' the monkeys said, 'and three of us. So we win!'

'You don't have to call *me* Hermione,' the penguin said as the argument raged on. 'You could call me—'

'*Silence!*' barked Aunt Severe, in a voice that made the lamps on the mantelpiece tremble.

Noone spoke. For a moment, even the penguin said nothing. Then he began waddling round the room, chattering away as happily as ever.

'How do you do?' he announced, bowing to

the armchair. 'My name's Silence. Silence the penguin.' He turned to the fireplace. 'Silence the penguin. At your service.'

Aunt Severe picked him up, popped the ping-pong ball onto his beak and tied it in place with the ribbon so he couldn't utter so much as a whisper.

'If you are going to argue about it,' she said, turning to the rest of the animals, 'you can *all* be called Hermione. And don't you dare complain if you don't know who I'm talking to.'

The penguin waddled around looking angry. The monkeys and the ostriches sat in the corner and sulked. Only the crocodile seemed happy.

'I've got a name!' he said. 'I've finally got a *real name!*'

Then he put his head on the carpet and stared sadly at the wall.

'Don't suppose anybody'll remember it, though,' he sighed.

13

A Strange Procession

Early the next morning, a little girl was sitting in the ticket office of the railway station when the doors opened and in walked two ladies with very big bottoms and very long necks. They were wearing baggy dresses made from curtains, wide straw hats, scarves and sunglasses.

When the little girl caught a glimpse of their feet, she turned to her mother and said, 'Mum, those ladies have birds' feet.'

'Ladies don't have birds' feet, dear,' said her mother without looking up from her magazine.

The next through the door was what looked like a little boy in a penguin suit. He was wearing a woollen cap and scarf, and a ping-pong ball on his beak.

'Mum,' she whispered, 'there's someone in a penguin suit with a ping-pong ball on his beak.'

'Penguins don't have ping-pong balls on their beaks, dear,' said her mother, turning the page of her magazine.

Behind the penguin came another small boy pulling a wooden crate mounted on roller skates. In it sat three small figures hunched inside three big anoraks with the hoods up.

'Mum,' said the little girl, 'I'm sure I just saw three monkeys in a crate. They were wearing anoraks.'

'Monkeys don't wear anoraks, dear,' said her mother, still not looking up.

The last person to enter was an elderly woman in a long grey overcoat and a big grey hat. In her right hand she held a walking stick. In her left she clutched the handle of a pink suitcase that looked just like a crocodile. The handle was held in place by sticky tape and the crocodile's head and tail drooped down sadly on either side.

'Mum,' said the little girl, 'that lady's got a suitcase that looks just like a sad pink crocodile.'

'Crocodiles aren't pink, dear,' said her mother, taking out a pencil and starting to do the crossword. 'And they certainly aren't sad.'

The elderly woman bought eight tickets to London and then led the strange procession out onto the platform. As it went through the door, the suitcase banged its head on the handle and the little girl distinctly heard it mutter, 'I thought that would happen.'

The little girl sat on her seat and decided not to tell her mum that the suitcase had just talked. Mums obviously didn't have very good imaginations and they certainly never noticed *anything* interesting at all.

14

The Princess of Sighs

When the train arrived, Aunt Severe found seats for the animals and Daniel at the end of an almost empty carriage. She put the crocodile into the luggage rack and sat down opposite them on the other side of the aisle.

'Sit still,' she commanded. 'Be quiet. And if you must speak to anyone before I can answer, be *polite!*'

As the train moved off, Daniel saw a famous lady from the TV at the other end of the carriage. She was reading a magazine with the words *Princess of S* on the cover. With Aunt Severe's permission, he went up and introduced himself. She told him her name was Mrs Bonniface

Stibbe and that she was an expert on toys. When he asked what she was reading, she showed him the cover of her magazine and he saw that it wasn't *Princess of S* but *Princess of Sighs*.

'Who's that?' he asked.

'Not *who*,' said Mrs Bonniface Stibbe, 'but *what*. The Princess of Sighs is a doll. She was made thousands of years ago in China, by Emperor Wei the Wonderful. She had golden hair, clothes of silk and silver, and eyes of the purest diamond.

'For centuries she passed from emperor to emperor and travelled with them wherever they went. But then she was inherited by Bu the Bored, who couldn't be bothered to look after her and gave her to a sultan, Suleiman the Sad. He gave it to *his* son, Selim the Sadder, who promptly lost her playing marbles with Gilbert the Gruff.

'Gilbert the Gruff was a very bad owner and the princess grew dilapidated. His brother, Ulrich the Untidy, used her to prop open doors and his daughter, Louise the Lazy, let her fall into a waste-paper basket one day and couldn't be bothered to pick her up. Claude the Clumsy inherited her and kept dropping her. Arthur the Angry crashed his toy cars into her. Then Imelda the Impatient came to the throne. She didn't like the doll and pulled off her feet and plucked out her diamond eyes. And that was when something very strange happened.

'Whenever the princess was near a breeze, the air would pass through her empty eye sockets and make a sound, ever so faint and ever so sad, just like somebody sighing. That impressed Imelda's daughter. Her name was Sarah the Sympathetic and she called the doll the *Princess of Sighs* and ordered everyone to look after her. And for years they did, until her grandson, Ferdinand the Forgetful took the throne. He was so absent-minded he couldn't even remember to eat his breakfast when he was hungry, so it wasn't long before he put the princess down one day and forgot where he'd left her. And that was the last anybody saw of her for two hundred and fifty years.

'But now,' said Mrs Stibbe, 'she's reappeared. She was found in somebody's attic. And starting tomorrow, she's going to go on display in the National Gallery in London. That's where I'm going. I'm going to make a programme all about her.'

'Is she valuable?' Daniel asked.

'I'll say!' said Mrs Stibbe. 'She's the oldest toy in the world! Finding her is a tremendous achievement!'

Daniel wasn't very impressed. He was much more interested in rescuing the Colonel than hearing about a doll hundreds of years old.

But just as he was about to ask another question, he heard a frightful racket behind him. Daniel spun round to see the penguin flying through the air and the conductor sitting on the floor of the carriage.

It seemed that while he'd been talking, the animals had got themselves into a terrible mess.

15
Tickets, Please!

It had all started not long after Daniel went to talk to Mrs Stibbe. Because it was warm in the train and because Aunt Severe was tired from all her work making disguises the night before, it wasn't long before she was fast asleep. Shortly afterwards, the door to the carriage opened and a lady pushing a refreshments trolley appeared.

'Good morning,' she said as she stopped beside what she thought was a boy in a penguin suit, two ladies in straw hats and a crate full of anoraks. 'Anything from the trolley? A cup of tea? A sandwich?'

'What do we do?' whispered an ostrich, looking very nervous.

A monkey repeated Aunt Severe's instructions. 'Be *polite*.'

So the ostrich asked, as politely as she possibly could, 'Do you have any pebbles?'

'*Pebbles*?' said the refreshments lady.

'We don't have any teeth, you see,' the ostrich explained, 'so we swallow the pebbles and they grind up what we eat in our stomachs. And have you got any locusts? We *love* locusts!'

That was when the penguin, who'd been struggling for ages to get rid of the ping-pong ball, finally succeeded. He threw it into the crate and started talking.

'I like your trolley,' he said. 'Is it easy to push? Can I have a go? I bet I could push it all the way to the end of the train and back and not get exhausted once!'

Then the monkeys poked their heads out from their anoraks and asked if she had any bananas.

This was too much for the refreshments lady. She dashed off to find the conductor.

The ostriches and the monkeys wanted to wake up Aunt Severe or get Daniel, but the penguin told them not to bother.

'*I* can think up a story,' he said. 'I can talk us out of anything!'

He turned to face the conductor, who had now arrived and was standing beside them.

'You look like animals!' he said. 'We can't have animals on the train!'

'We're not animals!' the penguin replied. '*We* are members of the Antarctic Lamppost Delegation.'

'The what?' said the conductor.

'The government of Antarctica,' the penguin explained, 'is thinking about putting lampposts up all over the continent. It gets very dark down there in the winter, you know. But they're not sure which ones to use, so they've sent us to investigate. It's a really interesting job. We've been all over the world and looked at thousands of lampposts. I like the orange ones best.'

The conductor peered at the ostriches, whose sunglasses and hats had fallen off, revealing their long necks and wide beaks.

'They look like ostriches to me,' he said.

'Don't be silly,' the penguin said. 'They're lamppost inspectors. They can inspect every inch of any lamppost you show them. From the bottom, right to the very top. That's why they've got such long necks. They're always being mistaken for ostriches.'

'And these three?' demanded the conductor, pointing at the monkeys, who stared back up at him with wide, nervous eyes. 'They've got furry faces. They must be animals.'

'Not at all,' said the penguin. 'They've just got colds at the moment, so they're wearing warm woolly hats. They specialise in lampposts in jungles. Their favourites are the blue ones.'

The conductor turned to the penguin. 'And who are you?'

'I,' announced the penguin proudly, 'am the Duke of Antarctica's butler. I dress like this because it reminds him of home.'

'Oh, really?' asked the conductor. 'And what's your name?'

'Silence,' said the penguin.

'Don't you tell me to be quiet,' said the conductor.

'But it is,' said the penguin. 'And my friends are all called Hermione. Isn't that interesting?'

The conductor was now thoroughly confused and didn't know what to do. So in the end he just inspected their tickets and walked off. The animals sighed with relief.

Then the penguin ruined it all.

'I knew he'd never guess we were *real* animals!' he cried, jumping up and down and flapping his flippers triumphantly. 'I knew I could talk us out of trouble.'

The conductor heard every word and came running back.

'And *I* knew *I* was right!' he cried, seizing the penguin in both hands.

The ostriches shrieked and shot out their necks. This knocked the crocodile from the luggage rack and he landed with such a crash on the table that all the monkeys leaped out of the crate. They grabbed the first thing they saw, which happened to be the conductor's legs. He lost his balance and sat down on his bottom with a bump. The penguin bounced free and waddled away to talk to the refreshments lady about her trolley. She took one look at all the chaos and pulled the emergency cord.

That was when Aunt Severe woke up and Daniel turned round. But it was too late for either of them to do anything. The train screeched to a halt and soon both they and the animals were standing on the grass beside the railway line. The conductor threw the crate after them, then went back and grabbed the crocodile, which he tossed into Aunt Severe's arms.

'And take your plastic crocodile with you!' he said as he slammed the door shut.

The train departed, leaving them all alone in the middle of nowhere.

A few minutes later, it began to rain.

'I thought that would happen,' said the crocodile.

16

The Penguin Confesses

As darkness fell, the rain continued to fall with it. Aunt Severe found a tree to sit under, but the animals didn't join her. They were ashamed about what had just happened, so they sat in the rain and got wet. Daniel sat beside them and tried to cheer them up.

'It's not your fault,' he said. 'It was my idea for you to wear disguises.'

'But it would have worked if we'd kept quiet,' said an ostrich.

'And if we hadn't panicked,' said a monkey.

'No,' said the penguin, in a sad little voice no one had ever heard before. 'You're wrong! It was *my* fault.'

Daniel started to reply, but he stopped when he saw what was happening to the penguin.

His skin was falling down.

The feathers on his head and neck and shoulders had grown thin and stretched, while the ones around his tummy and feet were piled up in big fat rolls. His flippers were three times their normal size and he squelched like a sponge whenever he moved.

When he saw everyone staring, he sighed and said, 'I thought you'd find out one day.'

He began to wriggle from side to side. Soon, a second penguin head popped into view. This was followed by two more shoulders and flippers and another tummy. And then there were two penguins instead of one: a thin, skinny penguin standing up and a plump, squidgy penguin lying on the ground.

The skinny penguin grabbed the plump penguin in his beak. It hung down like a wet towel. When he let go, it fell into the mud and stayed there.

'You see,' the skinny penguin said, 'I'm really just as useless as you. I catch cold all the time.

And a penguin who catches cold is a *really* useless penguin.'

As if to prove his point, he sneezed. Twice. The first sneeze shook him all over. The second one made him so dizzy he had to sit down.

'That's why everyone laughed at me,' he said. 'All the other penguins were off fishing and swimming while I just stood there on the rocks shivering and sneezing. I even got cold in the zoo. But when the dragons taught me the spell to talk People, I asked them if they'd say a spell to make this penguin suit. They did, and it was the first time I'd been really warm in ages.'

He sneezed again.

'I told a fib when I said I stayed to help you,' he continued. 'I stayed because I didn't want to go home with the other penguins. I wanted to live somewhere where nobody would laugh at me. It almost worked, too. But now Mr Colonel's been kidnapped, and we're lost, and your aunt's even angrier with us. And all because I couldn't keep my beak closed. I really have made a *terrible* mess of things.'

He shivered and shook so much that the ostriches wrapped him in their wings to keep him warm and the crocodile sat on his feet to keep them dry. Using their tremendous grips, the monkeys squeezed all the water out of the penguin suit. The penguin put it back on and said no more.

Then they all sat in the rain and went on feeling useless.

A few minutes later, though, one of the ostriches stretched out her neck to shake off the rain. She stopped and pointed with her beak.

'I can see a light!' she said. 'Over there!'

Everyone else looked, but they couldn't see a thing. So Daniel climbed up the tree that was sheltering Aunt Severe and peered off into the distance.

'I can see it, too!' he called out. 'I think it's on top of a house.'

All at once, everyone's spirits lifted. If there really was a house, there was probably somewhere to shelter. Aunt Severe stood up. She told the animals to form a line and then, with Daniel leading the way, they all set off.

The last to leave was the penguin. He was about to follow when he stopped, turned round and hunted through the contents of the wooden crate until he found the ping-pong ball. Sliding it all the way onto his beak, he waddled off to catch up with the others.

17
Two Unlucky Ducks

On and on the little procession trudged, wading across ditches, struggling through brambles and winding its way between the dripping trees. After an hour, everyone was wetter than ever and covered from head to foot in mud.

But they had reached their destination.

Before them stood two gates. The gap between the gates was filled with flickering red laser beams. On the far side, a long wooden bridge stretched across a gloomy and forbidding lake to a gloomy and forbidding castle. The light Daniel had seen shone from a tiny window at the top of a tall tower. Every other window in the building was as dark as a bottomless well.

Beside the gates was a sign. The words were easy for all to read.

DANGER!

DANGER!

DANGER!

DO NOT ENTER!

Trespassers will be tied up, locked up and dealt with **ruthlessly!**

At the bottom, in smaller letters, was a list of instructions. Aunt Severe stepped closer to read them out.

1. Do not open gates until unlocked from inside.

2. Do not cross grass between gates until laser beams are switched off.

3. Do not cross bridge until trembling device is switched off.

4. Do not open door until computer completes voice identification.

As she was standing there, two ducks flew out of the trees and landed on the grass between the gates, right in the middle of the laser beams. Sirens blared and alarm bells clanged. The ducks shot away to take refuge on the bridge.

But the second their feet touched the wooden planks, the bridge shuddered and shook and turned upside down. If the ducks hadn't been able to fly, they would have been dumped straight into the icy waters of the lake. They flew to the castle and landed before the front door. A mechanical voice boomed out from a loudspeaker above them.

'STATE YOUR NAME!' it commanded.

'VOICE IDENTIFICATION WILL FOLLOW IMMEDIATELY!'

The ducks quacked and clattered in Duck.

'VOICE UNKNOWN!' the loudspeaker blared out. 'TRESPASSERS WILL BE PUNISHED!'

A trapdoor snapped open beneath them and the ducks vanished from sight, leaving nothing behind but feathers.

Aunt Severe watched all this in silence. Just as she was about to return to the others, she noticed the final instruction at the very bottom of the sign.

5. Now step back quickly!

'Why on earth should I do that?' she wondered.

A second later, she found out.

A door in the side of the castle sprang open and a long metal arm with a net at the end snaked across the water. It scooped her up and shot back into the castle. The door slammed shut with an ear-splitting clang.

As silence fell once more, the crocodile turned to his companions.

'I thought that would happen,' he said.

18
Daniel's Plan

The animals sat and stared at the spot where Aunt Severe had vanished. They were even more discouraged than ever.

Daniel wasn't discouraged at all. He walked up to the gates and examined them. Then he studied the laser beams. After that, he looked at the bridge and the door of the castle. And finally, he smiled.

'I know how to get in,' he said and began to explain his plan.

'We can't do *that*!' the animals said when he'd finished. 'We're useless. Remember?'

'No, you're not!' Daniel. 'You just don't do what you're good at. What we need is someone who's tall enough, flat enough, strong enough *and* talkative enough to make it work. I can't do any of those things. But *you* can. You're *exactly* the right ones for the job. And I know you can do it!'

The animals remained unconvinced. Until the crocodile spoke.

'Daniel's right,' he said. 'If we don't rescue Aunt Severe, we can't rescue Mr Colonel. And Mr Colonel was really nice to us. He never laughed at us because we were useless. But if we don't rescue him, that's what we will be: *useless*. And I'm fed up with being useless!' he finished.

With that, he got up and walked over to the gates. A few seconds later, trembling all over, the other animals joined him.

And Daniel's plan began.

19
Very Odd Burglars

On Daniel's command, and ever so carefully, the ostriches slid their long, slender necks through the bars of the gate and looked around until they spotted a small switch on one of the gateposts. When they pressed it with their beaks, the gate swung open.

Then it was the crocodile's turn. He stretched out on the grass and waited until Daniel said he was as flat as he could possibly go before beginning to crawl. He crawled all the way under the laser beams, which danced and flickered above him but never came low enough to touch so much as a scale on his back. When he reached the far side, he found a big lever and knocked it down with his tail. The laser beams vanished.

The ostriches poked their beaks through the bars of the second gate, found another switch and pressed it. The gate swung open and the monkeys stepped forward. Daniel went with them and held their hands until the very last moment. He was feeling nervous, too. But he was careful not to show it.

Taking three big deep breaths, the monkeys held tight to the railing and put their feet on the first plank. Immediately, the bridge turned upside down. But they didn't fall into the lake. They clung to the railing and hung in the air with their tails in the water, waiting until the bridge turned the right way up again. When it did, they took another step forward and repeated the whole process all over again.

Step by step and plank by plank, they made their way across the lake until they reached the paving stones before the castle's front door. There they found a switch. When they pressed it, the bridge stood still and Daniel and the other animals ran across to join them.

And then it was up to the penguin.

He plucked the ping-pong ball from his beak and stepped up to the voice identification computer. The mechanical voice that had greeted the ducks boomed out.

'STATE YOUR NAME!' it commanded loudly. 'VOICE IDENTIFICATION WILL FOLLOW IMMEDIATELY!'

'Hello,' said the penguin, 'I'm the penguin. My name's Silence.'

'VOICE UNKNOWN!' the computer announced in response. 'TRESPASSERS WILL BE PUNISHED!'

The trapdoor snapped open. But the penguin was ready for that and he stepped to one side to avoid falling in. When it closed, he went back to the microphone.

'Is it an interesting job?' he asked. 'Checking voices? How many do you recognise? I can recognise hundreds. Thousands, in fact. That's because when penguins get together, there are so many of us and we all look the same, and it would be impossible to tell one of us from the other if we didn't all have our own absolutely unique voice. So as long as we listen carefully, we'll always be able to find whoever we're looking for. Isn't that interesting?'

'VOICE UNKNOWN!' the loudspeaker boomed once more. 'TRESPASSERS WILL BE PUNISHED!'

The penguin stepped back while the trapdoor opened and closed, then returned to the microphone.

'What do you do when you're not checking voices?' he asked. 'Does it get lonely? Do you have any friends? Can you talk to other computers? Or don't you like talking? I like talking. I think it's almost as much fun as eating. What do you like to eat?'

On and on he went, talking about icebergs and rocks and what he was going to do on his holidays. The night wore on. The rain stopped falling. Daniel decided to sit down. Then the crocodile stretched out on the grass and closed his eyes. The monkeys curled up beside him and the ostriches laid their heads on each other's backs. Soon they were all fast, fast asleep.

And still the penguin went on talking.

'And then one day I ate a blue fish,' he said. 'Most fish are silver, but this one was blue. It was ever so tasty. Almost as tasty as—'

Without warning, sparks shot out of the loudspeaker and the screen flashed red and yellow and green and blue all at once.

'STOP!' the computer pleaded. 'I GIVE UP! YOU CAN GO IN! I DON'T RECOGNISE YOUR VOICE AT ALL BUT YOU CAN GO IN! I'LL EVEN OPEN THE DOOR FOR YOU! BUT PLEASE STOP TALKING! I JUST WANT YOU TO STOP *TALKING!*'

And with that, the front door swung silently open to reveal a dark and empty hallway.

Daniel's plan had worked.

20
A Terrible Apparition

Slowly and hesitantly, the little group stepped inside, only for all of them to watch in horror as the door swung shut behind them the moment they crossed the threshold. Daniel's heart pounded in his chest as he peered into the shadows that stretched before them. But he didn't say anything. The animals had all been brave. Now he would have to be brave, too.

He took one cautious step forward. And then another. When he took his third step the animals followed him. On they went, making their way through echoing corridors and massive, empty rooms. Every corner was thick with cobwebs. Dust covered the floors in drifts. After several minutes, they reached a narrow spiral staircase that wound all the way up to a door under the roof.

'What a gloomy place!' said an ostrich.

'Who'd want to live here?' wondered the monkeys.

An answer wasn't long in coming. At the top of the staircase, a door swung open and a terrible apparition emerged. It had massive horns, gnarled claws and shoulders so broad it had to turn sideways to get through the door.

'*WHO ARE YOU?*' it boomed, in a voice that made the windows rattle.

The animals were terrified. As the ghastly figure began to descend the staircase, they huddled even closer together and didn't even dare breathe.

But halfway down, the giant stopped. One of its claws had got caught in the banisters and it had to tug and tug to pull it free. Suddenly, with a sound like a cork being pulled from a bottle, the claw flew off in one direction and the giant flew away in the other.

Down the steps it tumbled, and as it tumbled it

cried, '*Eek!*' and '*Aaah!*' and '*Oww!*' The animals saw a huge cloak come loose and fly through the air. The horns came hurtling after it. With a thump and a clatter, the giant came to a halt in the dust right in front of them.

'Ohhhh!' it wailed in a sad little voice. 'That *hurts!*'

Very slowly, it stood up and dusted itself off and the animals saw that it wasn't a giant at all. It was just a tall, gangly woman in a long overcoat.

'Have you come to laugh at me, too?' she asked in a deeply gloomy voice.

Daniel explained that they had come to rescue his aunt. 'Is she all right?' he asked.

'Oh, yes,' came the reply. 'I only locked her up so she wouldn't laugh at me.'

'Why would she laugh at you?' asked Daniel.

'Because everyone does,' the woman said. 'Don't you know who I am?'

Daniel and the animals shook their heads.

'That's to be expected,' she sighed. 'I suppose I was famous long before any of you were born. I'm Merly Stroop.'

And she proceeded to tell them her story.

21

Merly Stroop

Her real name, she said, wasn't Merly Stroop at all. She'd been adopted when she was just a tiny baby by the Stroopmoor-Stroopmoors. They were very rich and had more than plenty of everything, so they'd decided their new daughter should have plenty of names. They called her Macy Elizabeth Rosalyn Laura Yolanda Stroopmoor-Stroopmoor. And when they'd done that, they decided that she was going to be very, very famous.

From the moment she could crawl, they hired the best and most expensive tutors for private lessons in dozens of subjects. She had no brothers or sisters to distract her, and she wasn't allowed to play with other little boys and girls outside the house, or even to talk to the servants. She was permitted to do nothing but study.

And study she did, from sunrise to sunset, as well as at the breakfast, lunch and dinner table and even sitting in the bath.

By the time she was four she could speak English, Russian, German and Spanish. When she was six she was fluent in Mandarin and Arabic. By her eighth birthday, she had read over seven hundred books, painted two hundred oil paintings and carved fifty sculptures. She could play eighteen different musical instruments and had memorised two hundred and ninety-two songs and thirty-five symphonies. But what she really liked to do was dance. And she was very, very, very good at it.

She could tap dance, break dance, waltz and tango. She could do the Twist, the Madison and the Top and Tail. She was an expert in Morris dancing, line dancing and ballroom dancing. There wasn't a ballet step in the world she hadn't mastered.

So her parents decided that *this* was how

their little girl would become world famous. First, however, they changed her name. Lots of names were fine for a child who had to have everything, but they weren't very good for a world famous star: too many names were difficult to remember. They took the first letter of each of her first names, put them together with Stroop to make Merly Stroop, and proceeded to make her famous.

By the time she was nine, she was travelling the world giving dance recitals to packed auditoriums.

In between, she gave private performances for kings and queens and prime ministers by the dozen. Soon she had a television show, watched by millions. When she was ten, she began to make films.

The films were very simple. They were always about a little girl – plunged into thrilling adventures in strange locations all over the world – who danced her way to safety every time. She danced beside waterfalls in China, in a submarine under the Pacific Ocean, on top of an airplane over Iceland and even perched on a platform on the side of a skyscraper in Paris.

Audiences loved her. Millions went to her films and bought her DVDs. By the time she was ten and a half, there probably wasn't a person alive who hadn't heard of Merly Stroop.

And then disaster struck.

22
Useless As Well!

'What happened?' asked a monkey.

'I started to grow,' said Merly Stroop.

'Everybody does that,' said the crocodile.

'Yes,' said Merly. 'But I grew in leaps and bounds. In just a few weeks I went up inches. In months, a whole foot. Before anyone knew it, I was as tall as I am now and I was only twelve. And you look very odd when you're as tall as I am if you're only twelve. Lots of people laughed at me.'

'We know what that's like,' the ostriches said.

'But couldn't you still dance?' asked the crocodile.

'No,' said Merly. 'Because the more I grew, the clumsier I got,' she said. 'I started losing my balance and knocking things over and falling down. People started laughing at me for being clumsy.'

'We know what that's like,' the monkeys said.

'And I kept catching cold,' she continued. 'I never seemed to get warm unless I put on loads and loads of extra clothes. I think I was just too thin. That's why I have this overcoat on now.'

'I know what that's like,' the penguin said.

'Soon everybody said I was the strangest looking thing they'd ever seen in their lives: a big, tall, clumsy girl who was always sneezing and bumping into things. They said I didn't look like Merly Stroop at all. Then they started saying that I couldn't be Merly Stroop. They said nobody who looked as strange and silly as me could possibly be Merly Stroop and they laughed at me whenever I went on stage. They said I had to be the silliest thing absolutely anywhere in the world.'

The crocodile rested his nose on the ground and sighed.

'I know what *that's* like,' he said.

'So one day,' Merly went on, 'I ran away. I bought this castle and locked myself up inside so nobody would ever laugh at me again. I had plenty of food, excellent security and everything else I needed so I never had to leave. And it worked! Nobody ever laughed at me again!'

'Sounds *wonderful*!' the animals cried in unison.

Merly's face fell.

'But it *isn't*,' she sobbed. 'It's cold here. And lonely! Nothing ever happens. Nobody nice visits. Not even the Stroopmoor-Stroopmoors. When I stopped being famous, they didn't want to have anything more to do with me. You're the first friendly people I've spoken to since I arrived. All the others who came just wanted to laugh at me.'

'But you tried to frighten us away,' the crocodile said.

'I was frightened, too,' Merly explained. 'But now I've talked to you, I'm not.' Then she paused. 'There's one thing I don't understand. Why are you dressed up as animals?'

'Because we *are* animals,' the crocodile said.

One by one, they told her their stories.

'How awful,' said Merly when they'd finished. 'But I have to say, I loved Africa! I made a film in Africa,' she said in a dreamy voice. 'At the foot of the Mngong Hills. I stayed in a wonderful hotel and had a smashing time. I'd love to go back.'

'Why don't you?' the animals asked.

'No one to go with,' she said. 'That's the trouble with hiding away from the world: after a while you end up worse than when you started. I don't recommend it.'

Daniel, who had listened to every word of her story, felt just as sad for her as the animals did. He wished there was something he could do to help. And that was when he had an idea. Perhaps they could help each other.

'Why don't you come with us?' he said. 'To rescue the Colonel.'

He told her all about the Colonel and the toy thieves and how they'd ended up outside her castle.

'What an adventure!' cried Merly. 'And what rotten toy thieves! Of course I'll help. I'd *love* to help!'

'We'll need new disguises,' Daniel said, 'to get into the National Gallery.'

'I've got tons of old clothes,' said Merly. 'Take what you like.'

'And we still have to get to London.'

'We can go in my car,' said Merly. 'I never learned how to drive it, but if you were all clever enough to get in here, I'm sure *that* won't be a problem. Oh, meeting you is the most fun I've had in ages and ages!'

And before anyone could say another word, she rushed off to release Aunt Severe and the ducks. As the animals watched her depart, they were all thinking exactly the same thing: *How are we going to drive a car?*

23

PC Popperton

The very next morning, PC Popperton was riding his motorbike up and down the road leading to London, making sure the traffic was moving smoothly. He was a very happy policeman. Until he met the yellow limousine.

It was a massive car, with eight wheels instead of four, three rows of seats and a huge open sunroof. It was also absolutely filthy and looked as though it hadn't been cleaned in years. Twigs and dust and cobwebs covered every inch of it. But it wasn't the state of the car that astonished PC Popperton.

It was who was driving.

Perched on the middle seat with their heads

poking up through the sunroof were two ostriches with enormous necks. As he watched, they shouted to somebody inside the car.

'Left turn coming up! Then straight for a while.'

Standing on the front passenger seat was a penguin. When the ostriches shouted down through the sunroof, he repeated what they'd said to the three monkeys sitting in the driver's seat. One was holding the right side of the steering wheel, one the middle and one the left. The monkey on the left pulled down on the wheel

to turn the car in that direction. Then the other monkeys pulled back to make the car go straight.

The penguin saw PC Popperton riding alongside and waved.

'Hello!' he said. 'Is that a motorbike! Is it easy to ride? Could I have a go? It looks really interesting.'

This was too much for PC Popperton. He ordered the limousine to a stop and strode up to the rear window. Sitting in the back were an elderly woman, a small boy and the famous

dancer Merly Stroop. She was writing *I must not let my car get so dirty* five hundred and forty-two times. The small boy was writing *I must rescue my aunt much more quickly* nine hundred and twenty-seven times.

PC Popperton had been surprised by the animals. Now he was even more surprised to be standing right next to Merly Stroop because he'd been a big fan of hers when he was a little boy. But he told himself to be sensible and act like a proper policeman.

'Is this your car, madam?' he asked.

'Oh, yes,' said Merly.

'Are you aware that it's being driven by a penguin, two ostriches and three monkeys?'

'Don't forget the crocodile,' said Merly. 'He'll be ever so upset if you do.'

PC Popperton looked into the front and saw a pink crocodile lying on the pedals.

'What's he doing down there?' he demanded.

'Working the brakes and the accelerator, of course,' said Merly.

She handed over her lines to the elderly woman, who told her to write *I must learn to drive my own car* seven hundred and fifty-six times.

'Right,' said PC Popperton, feeling very confused as he took out his notebook. 'I'll have to make a report. I'll start with your names.'

But when he'd written them down, he felt even more confused. So he radioed the police station. The inspector answered.

'Um, I've just stopped a car, sir,' said PC Popperton.

'What's so strange about that?' said the inspector.

'It belongs to Merly Stroop,' said PC Popperton.

'Don't be ridiculous,' said the inspector. 'Nobody's seen Merly Stroop in years. She vanished ages ago.'

'She's sitting right in front of me, sir, in the back seat.'

'Then who's driving?' the inspector demanded.

'A penguin, sir.'

'I see,' said the inspector. 'And what's this penguin's name?'

'Silence.'

'Don't tell me to be quiet!' said the inspector.

'That really is his name, sir,' said PC Popperton.

'He listens to two ostriches looking through the sunroof. They're called Hermione. They tell him what's coming up and then he tells the monkeys behind the steering wheel which way to turn it. They're called Hermione, too.'

'I see,' said the inspector, sounding increasingly exasperated. 'And who's working the pedals? An elephant called Hermione?'

'No, sir,' said PC Popperton. 'A pink plastic crocodile. But his name *is* Hermione.'

'Popperton,' the inspector sighed, 'I've never heard anything quite so ridiculous in my entire life. You've obviously been working far too hard and you need a rest. Go right home this minute. I'll call your mother and tell her you're coming!'

PC Popperton put down his radio and told the animals they could drive on. They all thanked him and waved as they drove away. Then he climbed onto his motorbike and rode home to his mum. She made him a nice cup of cocoa, tucked him up in bed and gave him his favourite teddy bear from when he was little.

And then he felt much, much better.

24

Merly and the Giant

Later that same day, as PC Popperton lay in bed dreaming of talking penguins, a group of strange-looking characters climbed the steps leading to London's National Gallery.

One was a very tall elderly woman wearing a big grey hat and an enormous cloak that trailed along the ground. It looked as if it had been made from dozens of overcoats. In her right hand was a walking stick as tall as most adults and decorated with three monkeys. Behind her walked a thin woman with a scarf around her neck that looked just like a pink plastic crocodile. Beside her walked a small boy carrying a toy penguin under his arm.

The three of them entered the gallery and

walked through the wood-panelled corridors and hushed, high-ceilinged rooms crammed with paintings from every century. Finally, they reached their destination. There, in a large room and all alone in a small glass case on a tall marble pedestal, was the Princess of Sighs. Guards and thick red ropes surrounded the pedestal.

The very tall woman stepped forward to take a closer look.

And disaster struck.

The entrance was smaller than all the others in the gallery and the tall woman banged her head against the lintel. She swayed from side to side and then, before her companions could stop her, lost her balance and crashed to the floor.

The guards raced forward to help. But they stopped when they saw that she was actually a normal-sized lady standing on the backs of two ostriches and that the monkeys decorating the walking stick were real.

'Burglars!' they shouted. 'Call the police!'

What happened next took Daniel, Aunt Severe, Merly and all the animals completely by surprise.

Especially the crocodile.

25

A Very Happy Crocodile

When Aunt Severe, the ostriches and the monkeys tumbled to the ground, Merly jumped in surprise and the crocodile came loose from her neck. He landed on his back with a bump that dislodged the suitcase handle – still taped to his back – and sent it flying into his mouth.

He sprang to his feet and ran around and around in circles, opening and closing his jaws and doing everything he could to cough the handle loose. When he finally succeeded, it flew out onto the floor in front of the advancing guards. They stopped in their tracks and stared.

'That crocodile just ate a whole suitcase!' said a guard. 'All that's left is the handle!'

'Don't be silly,' said another guard. 'That's no crocodile. It's pink! And plastic!'

The crocodile's shoulders slumped yet again in disappointment. That made Daniel angry. He knew the animals weren't useless and he was fed up with people thinking they were. So he leaped onto a bench and shouted at the top of his voice: 'Oh no, it isn't! It's a *Crocodilius Pinkus*! It's the most dangerous crocodile in the world!'

'But its teeth aren't even sharp,' said a third guard.

'That's because it's worn them all away from chewing up suitcases,' Daniel said. *'And* the people carrying them!'

The guards' faces turned pale. Their knees began to tremble. When the crocodile coughed again, to get rid of a piece of sticky tape, they turned and roared off down the corridor, shouting and waving their arms.

'Run away!' they yelled. 'Run away! There's a *Crocodilius Pinkus* on the loose!'

The crocodile watched them go.

'I'm frightening,' he said, shaking his head in amazement. 'I'm really frightening! I never, ever, thought *that* would happen!'

Just then, two guards popped their heads round the corner to see if he was still there. When the crocodile took a step towards them, they shot back out of sight.

'*Crocodilius Pinkus* is still coming!' they yelled. 'Keep running away!'

The crocodile smiled the most enormous crocodile smile and shot off down the corridor.

'Oh,' he cried as he galloped away, 'you don't know how *happy* this makes me!'

Within minutes, the only ones left inside the National Gallery were Aunt Severe, Merly Stroop, Daniel and the other animals. And in the silence that followed, none of them missed the sound of footsteps on the roof, directly above the Princess of Sighs.

26

Rescued!

The roof was made of glass and, as Daniel looked up, he saw shadowy figures carefully remove a pane of it. A moment later, two small hands appeared, followed by a small body dressed in a green suit, a bright yellow waistcoat and a blue bow tie.

'Fry my fishcakes!' the Colonel muttered. 'Now I'm upside down!'

He was being lowered from the roof by a thick rope tied to his ankles. Holding onto the rope were Lionel Lurk and Sidney Slither. They stopped him just above the glass case.

'Grab the case,' they whispered. '*And* the toy! We'll pull you back up.'

That was when the ostriches dashed forward.

'You're not stealing Mr Colonel!' they cried, shooting out their necks and closing their beaks around his wrists.

'Flatten my hat!' the Colonel exclaimed as he caught sight of all his rescuers. 'You've come to save me!'

Lionel Lurk and Sidney Slither immediately began pulling the rope back up. Since they were much stronger, the ostriches' necks were soon stretched to their limit.

So the monkeys sprang to the rescue.

Leaping into the air, they wrapped their hands around the Colonel's hands, their feet around the ostriches' necks and held on tighter to both than they'd ever held onto anything before.

A furious tug of war ensued, with Lionel Lurk and Sidney Slither on one end, the monkeys and the ostriches on the other and the Colonel right in the middle. Back and forth he went, like a tree branch in a gale. Just as it looked as though the thieves might win, Daniel ran to the ostriches, put his hands against their chests and pushed with all his might. A moment later, Merly joined him and did the same.

The ostriches slid backwards, the toy thieves lost their grip and the Colonel came flying down through the air. Daniel tried to catch him, but Aunt Severe was quicker. She shot out her arms, caught the tumbling Colonel and clasped him tight.

'My darling!' she cried, smiling for the very first time since he'd disappeared. 'I've got you back again!'

'Dust my book shelves!' the Colonel replied. 'I always knew you'd rescue me, Emily.'

She rushed him away to safety in a corner.

The toy thieves fell, too, but there was nobody to catch them. They landed with a terrible crash of breaking glass right on the case containing the Princess of Sighs. She didn't break, though. She flew up into the air and then, by a terrible coincidence, tumbled all the way down into the outstretched hand of Sidney Slither.

He jumped up and dashed for the exit with Lionel Lurk close behind. But they didn't get far because coming the other way was the crocodile.

As soon as he saw them he opened his mouth and roared: 'I'm *Crocodilius Pinkus*, the most dangerous crocodile in the world! And I'm not useless at all!'

The toy thieves skidded to a halt in shock. Before they could move, the ostriches had wrapped their necks around their shoulders and the monkeys had used their tails, legs and arms to immobilise their ankles. The thieves were trapped and could do nothing to stop Daniel plucking the Princess of Sighs from Sidney Slither's hand.

For a moment, silence fell on the corridor. And in that silence, Daniel heard the faintest of sighs as the breeze from the missing window pane in the roof wafted over his hands and the princess. It was indeed a very sad, lonely sound, so sad and lonely it made Daniel cradle her extra gently and hold her safe until he could hand her back to the curator of the National Gallery. All this time, he'd only wanted to rescue the Colonel. But at that moment he was just as glad he'd managed to rescue the princess from the clutches of Slither and Lurk.

Then the corridor filled up with constables and sergeants, inspectors and superintendents, chief inspectors and chief superintendents. Some police dogs came, too, but the crocodile growled at them and they all ran away.

As the toy thieves were handcuffed and led away, the police started congratulating everyone and shaking hands all round. But they stopped as a loud voice boomed out. It was the Chief Superintendent.

'What about the *third* thief?' he demanded. 'He must be here somewhere. Everybody look for the third toy thief!' he commanded. '*Immediately!*'

And that was when the penguin came to the rescue. He hurried off into the corner where Aunt Severe and the Colonel were sitting, wriggled out of his penguin suit and handed it to the Colonel.

'Put this on,' he said, already starting to shiver. 'Then nobody will recognise you.'

The Colonel did as he was told. The suit was a perfect fit.

'Dip my socks in marmalade!' he exclaimed as he looked down at himself. 'Now I'm a penguin!'

The disguise worked perfectly. With all the animals and police in the corridor, nobody took any notice of an extra penguin. And then dozens of reporters arrived, all wanting to know how the toy thieves had been captured. Daniel told the story in detail, taking great care to say that he couldn't have done it without his aunt, or Merly Stroop, *or* the animals. As he spoke, his picture went out on dozens of TV channels all over the city. Two people in particular saw it, stopped what they were doing and raced to the National Gallery.

It was his mum and dad, and they were so happy to see him, they gave him the most enormous hug.

Shortly afterwards, one of the policemen shyly asked Merly Stroop if she would sign his notebook. She said yes and soon everyone was lining up to have their picture taken with her and get her autograph.

When she was finished, she even did a little dance for them.

And nobody laughed for a second.

27
Off to Africa

It was early the next morning when the yellow limousine – with Daniel's mum driving this time – pulled up in front of the castle. As everyone climbed out, they stopped and stared at the Colonel, who was now twice as large as the penguin and getting bigger by the second.

'Set my umbrella on fire!' he exclaimed. 'The spell must be wearing off.'

'Good,' smiled Aunt Severe, giving him an extra big hug. 'Then there's more of you to cuddle.'

The last person to emerge from the car was Merly.

'Well,' she said, 'time for one last look.'

'Why?' asked Daniel. 'Where are you going?'

'Off to Africa,' she said. 'I'm going to sell this castle and buy that hotel at the foot of the Mngong Hills. When I was growing up, I never had a holiday, so I'm going to make it a hotel for children who've never had one, either. And,' she said, turning to the animals, 'I'd like you to come with me.'

They couldn't believe their ears.

'You want *us* to go?' the crocodile asked. 'What would we *do*?'

'Well,' Merly said, 'you'd be Head of Security. You'd keep us safe from crooks and ne'er-do-wells.'

'And us?' asked the ostriches.

'Maintenance,' said Merly. 'With those long necks of yours there wouldn't be an inch of our hotel – from the cellar to the rooftops – you couldn't inspect. You'd make sure everything stayed in tip-top condition the whole year round.'

The monkeys looked glum. 'I don't know what *we* could do,' they said.

'You'd be vital!' said Merly. 'Our hotel's going to have the best adventure playground anyone's ever seen and you'd be responsible for safety.

With you there to catch them, nobody's ever going to fall down and hurt themselves.'

Finally, she turned to the penguin.

'As for you,' she said, 'you can be the hotel's storyteller. There'll be lots of children to entertain and they'll need *lots* of stories. I can't think of anyone better for the job.'

The animals huddled together and whispered. Then they straightened up and turned to Merly.

'We'd love to go,' they said.

'Excellent!' said Merly. 'I'll start packing.'

As she set off across the bridge, the animals lined up in front of Aunt Severe and the Colonel.

'We're sorry for all the trouble we caused,' the crocodile said. 'We really didn't mean to.'

'I know you didn't,' said Aunt Severe.

'And you certainly made up for it by coming to the rescue,' added the Colonel. 'You should all be very proud of yourselves!'

At the back of the group, the penguin shyly held up his flipper.

'May I ask a favour?' he said to Aunt Severe.

'Of course,' she said.

'The others still want to be called Hermione. May I be called Hermione, too?'

Aunt Severe smiled her biggest smile yet.

'I would consider it an honour,' she replied.

Then both she and the Colonel strolled away with Daniel's parents. The animals were all alone with Daniel.

'We can't thank you enough,' the crocodile said. 'If it wasn't for you, we'd still be hiding in the Colonel's house feeling useless.'

'Ah,' Daniel replied, 'but if it wasn't for *you*, we'd never have got the Colonel back. And my aunt would still be severe. We all helped each other. I'm really going to miss you,' he finished, suddenly feeling very sad.

'We're really going to miss you, too,' the animals whispered, just as sadly.

Suddenly, the crocodile told them all to gather round and started whispering. The animals listened, then nodded. Then they turned back to face Daniel. They all looked a little nervous.

'Um, would you like to come and see us in

Africa?' the crocodile asked.

'When we get settled in?' the ostriches and the monkeys added.

'We'd like you to be our Guest of Honour,' finished the penguin.

'Can I bring my mum and dad?' Daniel asked. 'And my aunt and the Colonel?'

'Of course!' cried the animals. 'The more the merrier!'

'Then I'd love to!' Daniel said.

And, huddled up happily together, they all walked across the bridge and inside the castle for breakfast.